儿童情绪管理与性格培养绘本

DO MY BEST

做最棒的自己

胡媛媛 编

广东旅游出版社
GUANGDONG TRAVEL & TOURISM PRESS
中国·广州

图书在版编目（ＣＩＰ）数据

做最棒的自己 / 胡媛媛编. — 广州 : 广东旅游出版社, 2016.11
（儿童情绪管理与性格培养绘本）
ISBN 978-7-5570-0547-4

Ⅰ.①做… Ⅱ.①胡… Ⅲ.①儿童故事 – 图画故事 – 中国 – 当代 Ⅳ.①I287.8

中国版本图书馆 CIP 数据核字(2016)第 237815 号

总 策 划 : 罗艳辉
责任编辑 : 殷如筠
封面绘图 : 赵里骏
责任技编 : 刘振华
责任校对 : 李瑞苑

做 最 棒 的 自 己
ZUO ZUI BANG DE ZIJI

广东旅游出版社出版发行
（广州市越秀区建设街道环市东路 338 号银政大厦西楼 12 楼　　邮编 : 510030）
邮购电话 : 020-87348243
广东旅游出版社图书网
www.tourpress.cn
湖北楚天传媒印务有限责任公司
（湖北省武汉市东湖新技术开发区流芳园横路 1 号　　邮编 : 430205）
787 毫米 × 1092 毫米　16 开　2 印张　1 千字
2016 年 11 月第 1 版第 1 次印刷
定价 : 15.00 元

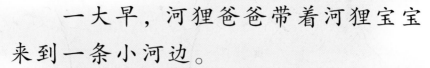

一大早，河狸爸爸带着河狸宝宝
来到一条小河边。

*In the morning, father beaver and
baby beaver came to a river.*

"爸爸，我们要干什么呀？"河狸宝宝好奇地问。

"Dad, what are we going to do?"
baby beaver asked curiously.

"当然是教你游泳呀。游泳是河狸的生存技能之一，你可要用心学哦！"河狸爸爸用期待的目光看着河狸宝宝。

"To train you to swim, for sure. Swimming is one of the survival skills of beavers, you must learn it by heart!" father beaver looked at baby beaver expectantly and said.

"好啊！"河狸宝宝回答。

"OK! " said baby beaver.

　　河狸爸爸是个游泳健将，河狸宝宝一直
希望自己能成为像爸爸那样的游泳高手。

*Father beaver was a great swimmer. Baby beaver
always wanted to be a good swimmer like his dad.*

可是，河狸宝宝看见一眼望不到底的河水，心里害怕极了。他想放弃，话到嘴边却怎么也说不出口。"不能让爸爸失望，我一定要学会游泳，我要做最棒的自己！"河狸宝宝给自己鼓劲。

However, looking at the deep river, baby beaver was so afraid. He wanted to give up, but hesitated. "I should not disappoint dad. I must learn to swim. I will do my best!" baby beaver encouraged himself.

"扑通"一声，河狸宝宝鼓起勇气，跳进了水里。

Baby beaver screwed up the courage and jumped into the river with a splash.

河狸宝宝站立不稳,倒在了水里。"啊……救……""命"字还没有喊出口,河狸爸爸已经将他抱出了水面。

Baby beaver could not stand still and fell off in the water. "Oh! Hel..." Father beaver had rescued him before he said the whole word.

"爸爸，我……我学不会游泳了。"受到惊吓的河狸宝宝低着头说。

"Dad, I... I don't think I can learn to swim."
Baby beaver felt frightened and lowered his head.

河狸爸爸摸了摸河狸宝宝的头，语重心长地说："你害怕的东西其实不在水里，而在你的心里。再试一次，你会有意想不到的体会哦！"

Father beaver touched baby beaver's head and said, "the thing that you are afraid of is not in the water; it's in your heart. Try again, you will get some unexpected experience!"

"我可不能退缩啊，爸爸对我的期望那么高，我怎么能让他失望呢！我再试一次吧！"河狸宝宝再次鼓起勇气。

"I can't shrink from it. D[...] has great expectations on me[...] can't disappoint him! Let's t[...] again!" Baby beaver had the courage again.

他正准备跳进河里，内心另一个声音却说："水那么深，刚刚如果不是爸爸，我可能就没命了！"

When he was about to jump into the river, there was a voice in his heart, "it is so deep. If dad had not saved me, I would have died!"

　　这时，又有一个声音说："不要怕，有爸爸在。要相信自己！"勇敢和害怕在河狸宝宝心中展开了激烈的搏斗。

Meanwhile, said another voice, "don't be afraid, dad is here. Trust yourself!" The braveness and the fear were fighting in his heart.

他咬咬牙，再次跳进水里，虽然呛了几次水，但他始终不放弃，努力练习着爸爸教的动作。

He gritted his teeth and plunged into the river again. Although he swallowed some water, he did not give up and practiced the actions learned from dad.

终于，河狸宝宝在水里游起来啦！它越来越喜欢在水里自由游动的奇妙感觉。

Finally, baby beaver could swim! He had come to love the free and wonderful feeling of swimming.

不久，河狸宝宝已经熟练掌握了游泳技能。

Soon after, baby beaver was proficient in swimming.

河狸宝宝在河里哼着歌,追着鱼,
别提有多开心了。

*Baby beaver was singing and chasing
fishes in the river. How happy he was!*

"爸爸，你看我学会游泳了，不会再害怕了。"河狸宝宝欢呼起来。

"Dad, look, I have learned to swim! I no longer fear the water," cheered baby beaver.

"你战胜了自己，你真棒！"河
狸爸爸开心地笑了。

"You defeated your fear. You are great!" father beaver laughed happily.

河狸宝宝望着爸爸，说："爸爸，我要像你一样，做最棒的自己。"

Baby beaver looked at dad, "Dad, I will be as good as you! I will always do my best! "

给父母的话：

　　无论哪个孩子，只要我们耐心寻找，就必定能发现他的优点，即使他（她）做错了事，我们也可以从中找到闪光点，关键是一个"爱"字。亲子之爱是基于血缘关系的本能的爱，是生命的原点，因此，父母对孩子的赏识与鼓励，是孩子"做最棒的自己"的关键。

　　就精神生命而言，每个孩子都是为得到赏识而来到人世间的，赏识教育的特点是发现并表扬孩子的优点和长处，让孩子在"我是最棒的孩子"的心态中最大限度地舒展自己的生命；相反，批评教育的特点是注重孩子的弱点和短处，使孩子在"我不行""我比别人差"的意念中沉沦。

　　每个孩子心中都有一个绘本中的河狸宝宝，他们既想勇敢地探索这个未知的世界，又因为认知能力有限而心中胆怯，这时做父母的就要帮助孩子战胜自己的弱点，让孩子与那一个体验了"成功"的河狸宝宝拥抱。

　　让孩子做最棒的自己，实质是承认差异，不怕失败，孩子一百次摔倒，父母要相信他能第一百零一次站起来，坦然面对生活中的挫折，用坚强的意志从失败中走向胜利。